Peggy
Porcupine

Peggy Porcupine

Dave and Pat Sargent

Illustrated by
Blaine Sapaugh

Ozark Publishing, Inc.
P.O. Box 228
Prairie Grove, AR 72753

F
Sar   Sargent, Dave and Pat
        Peggy Porcupine, by Dave and Pat Sargent.
        Illus. by Blaine Sapaugh.
        Ozark Publishing, Inc. 1996.
        38 P. illus.

        Summary: Peggy Porcupine knows she is
        supposed to play nearby, but she strays away
        from home and gets lost.
                    1. Porcupines. I.Sargent, Pat.
        II. Title. III. Series.

ISBN Casebound 1-56763-044-8
ISBN Paperback 1-56763-045-6

Ozark Publishing, Inc.
P.O. Box 228
Prairie Grove, AR 72753
Ph: 1-800-321-5671

Printed in the United States of America

Inspired by

my love for this amazing animal.

Dedicated to

my dear friend, Chad Goins.

Foreword

Peggy wanders away from home and meets another porcupine named Bob. Together, Peggy and Bob survive a frightening adventure, before being reunited with their mothers.

Contents

One   Climbing a Tree   1

Two   Getting Lost   13

Three   Home Sweet Home   23

Peggy
Porcupine

One

Climbing a Tree

Porcupines give birth to only one baby once a year. In March Mama Porcupine gave birth to a baby girl. She named her Peggy.

Peggy, an only child, got plenty of milk, and she grew like a weed.

Mama Porcupine and Peggy Porcupine lived in the bottom of a hollow tree. The entrance to their den was just above ground.

Peggy was about five weeks old when her mother said, "Peggy, it is time for you to start learning how to survive in the wilderness. You must also learn what is good to eat and what is not. There are many dangers lurking outside our den. I will teach you all you need to know to survive in the world outside. Your first lesson is tonight."

Peggy thought, "Oh, boy! I get to see what the world is like. I want to travel all over and see everything."

Mama Porcupine crawled through the small hole and called, "Come on, Peggy." Peggy wasted no time in crawling out of the den.

Mama Porcupine told Peggy if she got attacked, she should lie perfectly still and bristle her quills. She told Peggy that her quills were her only means of defense. Her quills were as sharp as needles, and they would be very painful to anything that touched them.

Mama Porcupine said, "The first thing we will do is get something to eat. There is a nice pine tree just down a ways. We'll climb it and eat some of the bark from the small, tender limbs."

Mama and Peggy made their way to the young pine tree. Mama Porcupine told Peggy, "Now you stay here and watch me climb the tree, and I will tell you when to start. Okay?"

"Okay, Mama," Peggy replied.

Mama Porcupine made her way up the tree with ease. She didn't seem to have any problem at all. She stopped and lay on a forked branch and said, as she looked down at Peggy, "Now it's your turn. Just take it slow and easy."

Peggy reared up against the tree and stuck her long, sharp claws into the bark. She started climbing the tree. She was a natural and had no problem at all. Once she reached her mama, her mama said, "Crawl out toward the end of this small branch and start peeling off the tender bark with your teeth. Now be careful and don't eat too much. It will give you a stomachache. As

you get older you will be able to
eat more."

Peggy crawled out near the
end of the limb and started eating
the tender bark. This was her first
taste of bark, and she thought,
"This is pretty good!" She ate quite
a lot, and then, remembering what
her mama said about not eating too
much, Peggy stopped eating and
started climbing all through the

tree, honing her skills as a climber.

To Peggy, this was all a lot of fun. She climbed up and down the tree and all through the branches. Finally, Mama Porcupine said it was time to go home. Peggy was having a lot of fun and wanted to play longer, but she also knew that tomorrow was another day.

That night while Mama Porcupine was fast asleep, Peggy was wide awake. She couldn't sleep. All she could think about was how much fun she had had that day. She wanted to go out and play on the trees again. She knew she wasn't to leave the den, but then thought, "It won't hurt if I go out and play nearby for just a little while."

Peggy crawled out of the den and climbed up a nearby tree. While she was high in the tree, she spotted another porcupine just a short distance away. She watched the porcupine for quite some time and then decided to take a closer look. Peggy climbed down the tree and slowly made her way toward the other porcupine. As she got closer, she saw that the porcupine was about her size.

She stopped a few feet away and looked at the young porcupine.

Peggy finally spoke up and said, "Hi. What's your name?"

"Bob," the young porcupine replied. "What's yours?"

"My name is Peggy," she answered, then asked, "Where do you live?"

Bob said, "I live in a den over by that big rock." Bob turned his

head in the direction of a large boulder. Peggy could see a hole in the ground beside it and knew that was his home.

Peggy then asked, "Do you come out alone often?"

"My mom lets me come out every day for just a few minutes, but I have to stay in sight of the den. How about you?" Bob asked.

"My mama was asleep and I wanted to play, so I just came out and that's when I saw you," Peggy answered. Then she asked, "Do you want to play for a while?"

"What will we play?" Bob asked.

"Let's climb trees. That's a lot of fun," Peggy answered.

Two

Getting Lost

Peggy and Bob started climbing up and down the nearby trees. They were having so much fun that they didn't notice they were getting further and further away from home.

After playing for a long time, they decided it was time to go home. They climbed down from the tree they were in and looked all around. They saw nothing that reminded them of home. They headed up the hill, hoping to see their homes just any minute. Little did they know, they were traveling in the wrong direction and each step took them farther and farther away. After a time, Peggy and Bob knew they were lost.

They stopped for a few minutes, and Peggy said, "I'm going this way," and headed down the hill toward the river. Bob hollered,

"Wait for me," and took off after her.

Peggy and Bob continued their journey down the hill until they

came to the river. They stopped at the river's edge and tried to figure out what to do next.

Peggy said, "I'm hungry and sleepy."

"Me, too," replied Bob.

Then Peggy said, "Let's eat some bark from one of these trees, and maybe we'll feel better."

"That's a good idea," Bob said, and the two of them climbed a nearby tree and started gnawing away at the bark. Peggy pulled a big piece of bark loose and started chewing on it. She started sniffing and sputtering and said, "Yuk! This is terrible! It's not at all like what I ate before. This is bitter and doesn't taste good."

"Mine doesn't taste good either," Bob replied.

"Do you think this is the wrong kind of tree?" asked Peggy.

"I don't know. It may be," Bob replied.

"Let's try another one," Peggy said, "and see if it's any better." The two of them climbed from the tree and found another small one nearby. They climbed to the top where the limbs were small and tender. They started eating the tender bark from the small limbs and found that the bark on that tree was just as bad as the bark on the first one. They continued from tree to tree only to discover that all the trees tasted just alike.

Peggy and Bob finally stopped and lay by the river's edge. Bob asked Peggy, "What are we going to do now?"

"I don't know," Peggy replied, "but we have to find food."

They both lay there in total silence for a long time. The silence was finally broken when Peggy asked, "When you were eating bark with your mother, what did it taste like?"

"It was sweet and juicy," Bob replied.

"That's what it was like when I ate it, too," Peggy stated. Then she asked, "What did the tree look like that you and your mother ate from?"

"Gee, I don't know. I never paid any attention. Just a tree, I guess," Bob answered.

"Well, we must be eating on the wrong kind of tree or something. Think real hard, Bob, and see if you can remember anything at all about the tree you ate from."

"Okay," Bob replied. And again they both lay there in total silence, trying to remember what kind of tree they had eaten on when they were with their mothers.

Peggy finally spoke up and said, "I remember Mama telling me we were going to eat some bark from a pine tree. But I don't know what a pine tree looks like."

"Yeah, it seems like I remember something about a pine tree, too," Bob replied. He continued, "If I remember right, Mama said a pine tree doesn't have leaves. It has needles that look like our quills, except they are green and not as stiff and sharp."

"Well," Peggy said, "let's see if we can find a tree like that."

The two of them headed up the river in search of a pine tree. They searched for a long time before finding one that looked like it might fit the bill. Peggy and Bob climbed to the top of the small pine and began eating the tender bark.

"This sure is good," Peggy said. "It looks like we finally found a pine tree."

"Yeah, and it's about time," Bob stated. "I was starved to death."

The two young porcupines had their fill of sweet, juicy pine bark and climbed from the tree and returned to the river's edge, where they once again lay in silence and drifted off to sleep.

Three

Home Sweet Home

After a long nap, the two little porcupines woke up. They were both sad, and they missed their mothers. Neither of the young porcupines had ever seen a big body of water before, and Peggy became very curious about it. She took her front paw and stuck it in the edge of the water. She immediately jerked it back. The water felt strange, and it made her paw wet. She looked at her paw and thought, "It didn't hurt," so she stuck her paw in the water again. This time, she noticed the water splash a little. She started splashing the water a little harder. She splashed water all over herself and Bob.

Bob just lay there watching all of this. The cool water felt good, and he decided to join in the fun.

Peggy and Bob splashed around in the water having a lot of

fun, and for a little while, they for-
got their loneliness.

There was a large dead log
sticking out in the water. It had
been washed downstream and was
caught on a rock at the edge of the
river. After getting tired of splashing water, Peggy crawled on top of
the dead log and slowly made her
way to the other end, which stuck
way out in the water. Whatever

Peggy did, Bob was going to do, so he was right behind her.

The swiftness of the water caused the log to rock a little, and the mild rapids caused it to bob gently up and down. The rocking and bobbing motion was like a merry-go-round. Peggy and Bob were having a lot of fun.

As Peggy and Bob ran back and forth on the log, a smaller log floated down the river. The small log bumped the end of the large log, jarring it loose from the rock it was caught on. The large log turned and floated away from the bank. It started bobbing up and down and rolling from side to side as it floated across the shallow rapids. The log caught on the jagged rocks, and Peggy and Bob lost their grip. Their fun had turned into fear. There was no way to get off of the log, and neither knew how to swim. Even if they could swim, the water was so swift in the rapids that they would be washed away. All they could do was hold on for dear life.

It was several minutes before the rocking, swaying, and rolling of the log slowed to a gentle rocking motion. They had survived the rapids. Now the river was much wider, and the water was very calm.

Up ahead was a large pile of sticks and limbs. The log was floating straight for it.

The young porcupines floated into a beaver pond, and the log they were on was heading straight for the beavers' lodge.

The log hit the edge of the beavers' lodge, then turned, coming to rest against the back of it.

Peggy and Bob had all of the log they wanted and scurried around trying to get off as fast as they could. The only place to go was on top of the beavers' lodge.

The pitter-patter of little feet on top of the lodge frightened the beavers.

Two beavers, Billy and Susie, lived inside. They thought their lodge was being attacked, so they swam from the lodge through their underground entrance. When they reached the surface, they saw the two young porcupines and knew what had happened.

Billy Beaver swam over to the lodge and asked, "Are your names Peggy and Bob?"

They both answered, "Yes!" at the same time.

Billy Beaver said, "Your mamas were just here looking for you. They said you were playing outside and had gotten lost."

"We did," Peggy answered. Then she asked, "Do you know where our mamas are now?"

"I'll see if I can catch them," Billy replied, as he swam toward the dam.

He climbed on top of the dam and hollered, "Hey! Over here! I found them!"

In just a couple of minutes, the two mama porcupines came running up the riverbank.

Billy Beaver had Peggy and Bob get back on the log, and he pushed the log to the bank. Peggy and Bob were reunited with their mothers, and they never wandered away from home again.

Porcupine Facts

A porcupine is an animal that has long, soft hairs and strong, stiff quills on its back, sides, and tail. Porcupine quills are long, sharp bristles of hairs that are fused (grown together). Porcupines defend themselves by striking attackers with their quilled tails. The quills come out easily and stick

into the attacker's flesh. The porcupine grows new quills to replace the lost ones. Porcupines cannot shoot quills at their enemies, as some people believe. In some kinds of porcupines, the tip of each quill is covered with tiny, backward-pointing projections called barbs. The barbs hook into the flesh, and the quills are difficult to remove. Porcupine victims may die from infections caused by germs on the quills, or from damage to a vital organ. Quills may even stick in an attacker's jaw, making the animal unable to open its mouth, thus causing starvation. Fishers, large members of the weasel family, attack porcupines by flipping them over onto their backs.

Porcupines are rodents (gnawing animals). Biologists classify them as Old World porcupines and New World porcupines. Old World porcupines live in Africa, south-eastern Asia, India, and southern

Europe. Most kinds of Old World porcupines grow about three feet long, including the tail. They make their homes in tunnels in the ground and do not climb trees.

New World porcupines live in North and South America. These animals spend much time in trees. Several South American porcupines, called *coendous*, can even hang by their tails. Only one kind, the North American porcupine, lives in North America. North American porcupines are about three feet long and weigh about twenty pounds. Their yellowish-white quills are two to three inches long. Their fur is brownish-black. North American porcupines live chiefly in forests of coniferous (cone-bearing) trees, such as pines and firs. They eat green vegetation and tree bark. They often climb trees to strip the bark from the upper part of the tree. This some-times kills the tree.

Female North American por-cupines give birth to a single off-spring in the spring. The babies have quills at birth. North American por-cupines are often incorrectly called hedgehogs. True hedgehogs live only in the Eastern Hemisphere. The flesh of the North American porcupine is edible, but few people consider it tasty.

Other books by Dave and Pat Sargent

Billy Beaver
Roy Raccoon
White Thunder
Redi Fox
Brutus the Bear
Dike the Wolf
Chrissy Cottontail
Dawn the Deer
Sammy Skunk
Bobby Bobcat

Big Jake
Tunnel King
Buddy Badger
Amy Armadillo
Barney the Bear Killer
Greta Groundhog
Mad Jack
Molly's Journey
Pokey Opossum
The Bandit